MaryJane Miller
271 South First Street
Dixon, CA 95620

DISTANT SERENADE

MICHAEL MCLEAN

ILLUSTRATED BY SCOTT SNOW

DESERET BOOK COMPANY,
SALT LAKE CITY, UTAH

To the women in my family—Lynne, Meggan, Martie, Merrie,
Joyce, Tracy, Moe, Ellie, Bradeigh, Kari, Jane, Kristin,
Nanny, Wisey, and Nona—and to all the women who have passed,
and will pass, the melody of their lives from generation to
generation to generation

THE STORY

THE SONGS

I'd like to thank the people who have helped make this book a movie. No, it's not in the theaters yet; it's a movie you'll be creating in your mind every time you read it and listen to the soundtrack that accompanies the book. To make this "mind movie" happen required the creative support of several gifted people, but there are two in particular I'd like to thank here.

Scott Snow's stunning illustrations are remarkably powerful storytelling pieces that not only capture the texture and tone of this story but also enrich it with symbolic insight. In any wonderful movie, every time you see it you discover something new, and that is also true with Scott's illustrations. I love the way he has incorporated into his artwork a symbolic representation of the melody that is in search of its identity. And I'm moved by the way his illustrations convey such a depth of human emotions while portraying so many nonhuman creatures.

I also want to thank John Batdorf, who co-produced the soundtrack to this book with me. His orchestrations brought the original songs I'd written for the story to vibrant reality. In addition, he composed, arranged, and performed all the transitional underscores that give *Distant Serenade* the feeling that you are indeed watching a movie.

I hope you will take the opportunity to "perform" *Distant Serenade* for someone you care about, or perhaps for someone you think might need to feel its message, even if it's just yourself. At the top of page 7, start the tape or compact disc and you'll hear the first few paragraphs narrated prior to the singing of the first song, "Tell Me Where I Belong." This will give you a sense of how the story is underscored. As the music continues to play, feel free to give the performance of a lifetime to whoever may be listening. And should you choose to sing the songs yourself, the music and lyrics are included in the back of the book.

There was a moment in the writing of this story and its accompanying songs when I saw all the faces of all the people who have touched my life, and I wanted to magically summon them to my studio and say to them, "This is about you, and you, and you, and you. How can I ever thank you for what the melody of your lives has meant to me?"

I hope this book and the music are a start.

Michael McLean

"Do you think I'm ready?"

It was barely a whisper.

If the old woman didn't answer, Ellie could always tell herself it was because she hadn't heard her.

There was a long pause.

Why is she taking so long? Ellie wondered. *She's not that* old. *Either she thinks I'm ready or she doesn't!* Ellie decided not to ask again. Not ever. If the old woman didn't want to tell her, fine. Ellie could live with that. After all she'd been through, what was one more disappointment?

"Look," she told her Aunt Louise, "you don't have to tell me if you don't want to. It's no big deal. I just . . . "

"You just what, Ellie?"

"Well, you said you had something you needed to tell me, but only when I was ready. And I was just wondering . . . I mean, if you don't want to, it's okay. But if you'd like to, I think I'm ready for . . . whatever it is you wanted to tell me but you couldn't because I wasn't . . . but I think, maybe, you know, like now I am." *My, my,* Ellie thought to herself, *you have such a way with words.*

A glance at her Aunt Louise's wrinkled face revealed that she was somewhere else, deep in thought. Ellie didn't have the patience to wait any longer for her response, so she walked down the hall toward the bedroom. She'd been told since she arrived to make herself at home, but she couldn't. Though some of her things were here, her heart wasn't. This wasn't her home. She didn't belong in this place, and she never would. But what made her feel worse was the truth piercing the center of her heartache: she had no feeling of belonging anywhere.

She looked out the window at the vast landscape surrounding her new Australian home, and it was as barren and forsaken as a distant planet in a science fiction movie. But her life was not a movie, though she often wished it was. In a movie her parents could have survived the accident, somehow. In a movie the nightmare of her life could be nothing more than a dream. In a movie she wouldn't have been forced to move to Australia to be with her only living relative, an anthropologist who had spent most of her life studying strange cultures of obscure peoples around the world. If Ellie's life were a movie, she would be pretty enough and confident enough and smart enough to make it on her own. She wouldn't need to live with this ancient guardian, a distant woman who knew nothing about the world Ellie lived in.

Lost, and feeling terribly alone, Ellie strained to feel her parents near. She tried to remember things they'd told her, advice they'd given, words they'd said. Anything. But their words didn't come. Her memories came only in the form of feelings, and what pained her more than anything else was the fear that she would never know those feelings again—hope, love, peace, and the sense of belonging somewhere and to someone. She felt the tide of feelings going out, forever, leaving nothing but an all-gone feeling around her heart.

Ellie's thoughts wandered aimlessly for a while and collided in the emptiness. And then she started humming. It wasn't a conscious thing where she picked a melody and gave it life. It was more like breathing. It came naturally, instinctively, from a place deep within.

The tune, soft as it was, floated down the hall until it found Aunt Louise. The melody caught the old woman unprepared, though not ungrateful for its arrival. It reached inside her and touched a tender part of her past. Louise lingered on the memories the melody brought to mind, and, had it been possible, she would have stayed in that place for some time. But as the melody wrapped itself around the old woman again and again, it created a sense of urgency. She couldn't sit there any longer, remembering. She *had* to tell Ellie! Hearing that melody coming from her niece down the hall, Louise knew, without question, that it was time. Ellie *was* ready.

A moment later Louise appeared in the bedroom doorway. "Come with me, Ellie," she said. "It's time."

The gentle command was like a magnet that pulled Ellie from the bed and toward her aunt. As she followed obediently down the hall and out the front door, she noticed that her aunt was walking with a livelier step than usual, impatient to get to wherever it was they were going. Louise jumped in the dusty old Land Cruiser and revved up the engine, like a teenager in a hurry. Almost before Ellie could close the rusty door, they were off.

A few miles down the red dirt road, the Land Cruiser started to stutter and backfire. Aunt Louise shook her head in frustration and muttered, "C'mon, Oscar, I don't have time for this!"

"Who's Oscar?" Ellie asked.

"The bucket of bolts we're riding in." Louise tapped quickly on the accelerator several times, but the truck just limped a few hundred more yards, backfired, and died.

"Why Oscar?"

"Oscar was the most frustrating man I've ever known." Louise smacked the steering wheel with both hands for emphasis. "And like an *idiot,* I thought I could count on him. But I couldn't. My luck with cars has been about as good as my luck with men, so I name my cars after 'em—and this undependable one I've appropriately named Oscar."

A frustrated Louise turned to Ellie for a response and saw a rather stunned look on her niece's face. Without knowing she was doing it, Ellie leaned closer to her Aunt Louise, ever so slightly, and looked quizzically into her face. Something was changing. Ellie would never be able to explain how, but she began seeing glimpses of someone very different from the weathered and worn anthropologist she called her Aunt Louise. She saw a girl, not too much older than herself, peeking out from behind that old, leather-skinned mask.

"Were there others—besides Oscar, I mean?" Ellie asked with genuine concern that caught Louise a bit off guard.

"Quite a few—couple of vans, several pick-ups, and a Jeep." Louise hoped to get more of a laugh from her niece than she did. Apparently her niece really wanted to know about the old girl's romantic past, such as it was. More seriously she said, "There were others, Ellie, but they never got to me the way Oscar did."

"You have a picture of him?"

"Of Oscar?" Aunt Louise smiled. "Yes, I have a picture of him."

"Could I see it?"

"I don't know if you could."

"How come?" Ellie asked.

"Because I keep it here." Louise pointed to her heart. Then she smiled warmly at her niece, got out of the ancient Land Cruiser, and started poking around under the hood.

"What about you, Ellie? Fallen for anyone yet?"

"Kind of," Ellie said haltingly.

"What do you call him?"

Ellie pictured Jason Campbell, the only boy she'd ever fallen for, and thought about the letters he'd never answered and all the times he'd let her down.

"Does he have a name?" Aunt Louise asked again.

"Yeah, he has a name," Ellie said with a touch of venom in her voice. "It's . . . Oscar!"

The tough old lady under the hood started laughing, and it was contagious. "You're all right, kid. You're all right!" And she put her arm around her niece. It felt good, for both of them, and it was there and then, next to a broken-down Land Cruiser named Oscar, that Ellie and her Aunt Louise bonded—not as relatives but as friends.

"Where have you been all my life, Aunt Louise?"

"Trying to find myself, I suppose."

Ellie thought it was an odd comment coming from a successful anthropologist. As they chatted, Louise was elbow deep in the engine and had managed to get a grease smudge on her chin.

"I don't think my mother knew very much about you, really. What happened?"

"Well, in the first place, Ellie, your mother was almost young enough to be my daughter. I was just starting college when she was born. But you know all this, right?"

Ellie had a vague recollection of hearing this before, but she wanted to hear it from Louise herself. "Go on," she said.

"Well, my father died when I was about your age. I had only my mother to hold on to during that time. But a few years later she remarried and decided to have a child with her new husband. I felt a bit abandoned, so I pushed to graduate from high school a year early and left for college. When your mother was born, I was off in another world, and I suppose to some degree I have been ever since."

"So you were half sisters?"

"Looking back, it was a lot less than even half, I'm sorry to say. It was just too painful, even as a grown woman. But I could bury myself in my work. And when I was learning about other cultures and other people, I didn't feel quite so lost."

The clanging of the wrench against the engine ceased. Louise rose from the jaws of the Land Cruiser with an announcement: "I've got some good news and some bad news. The bad news is, Oscar won't be taking us anywhere today. But the good news is, Oscar was thoughtful enough to break down a mile or two from home instead of thirty." She squinted and looked at the sky and then down the dusty road toward her home. "It's not that bad a walk. If we start now, we'll make it before it's too dark. Come on." She closed the hood of the Land Cruiser, grabbed a canteen and a jacket from inside, and started walking.

"Well, kid, this wasn't the setting I had in mind."

"Where were we going?" Ellie asked.

"To a special place of the Aborigines I've been studying. I thought it might help make what I'm going to tell you more vivid in your mind. It's an extraordinary place—rock paintings on huge expanses four hundred feet high."

"So I guess we'll have to wait?" Ellie said with a bit of disappointment.

"Absolutely not, my dear. I said it was time, and it is time. We'll just have to use a little extra imagination, that's all. Besides, it'll make the walk home more interesting."

They walked together a few hundred yards down the road, and nothing more was said. Ellie's eyes went back and forth between the road ahead and the profile of her aunt's face.

During this extended silence, her Aunt Louise was moving her lips as if rehearsing what she was about to say.

Finally she spoke: "Ellie, I think one of the main reasons I love my work is because I'm so moved by the stories of the people I study. These people have stories that have been passed on for hundreds and even thousands of years that have never been written down. The stories exist only as long as families tell them to each other. And the telling of these stories is the way these people discover who they are. It's how they connect one generation to the next. It's both their education and their entertainment. And sadly, as the modern world comes bullying its way into these cultures, the magic and wonder of their storytelling is being lost, and I'm afraid that once lost it may never be reclaimed."

Aunt Louise spoke with passion and concern that had grown bone deep through a lifetime of research.

"Through the years I think I've been jealous of these people and their stories. I was certain I had nothing special passed on to me that I could then pass on to the next generation. It took me all these years to figure out that I probably became an anthropologist because I've been hungering to be a part of something I never had myself."

Louise paused for a moment as if confirming to herself that what she'd just said was true.

"Well, a few months before the tragedy that brought us together, I was in the bush with some Aborigines for an extended time, and we became friends. One day, one of the older women of the tribe asked me what stories I would be passing on to my family, and I started to cry. The old woman said nothing, but a few days later she took me to the place I was hoping to take you today and said, 'I give you story. Then you have one for telling when daughter is ready.' When I told the woman I didn't have a daughter, she smiled and said, 'She coming . . . she coming.' "

Louise looked tenderly at Ellie and then continued.

"The woman gave me a story, like a precious gift, and vanished into the bush. After I got the wire about your parents' death and your coming to stay with me, I tried to find her, but I couldn't. I've thought of her and the gift she gave me almost hourly since you arrived, and I've been waiting and watching and preparing for the right time to pass this story on. The words I've chosen are mine, Ellie, but I so hope they can begin to convey the same spirit I felt when the story was given to me.

When the earth was ready to be born, the eternal Sky Dwellers felt a beckoning, and they came. Their coming stirred ancient Ancestors who lived beneath the crust of the unborn earth. Once awakened, these Ancestors stretched and yawned and stood on the surface and began to roam the planet. As they did, they sang, and with each new verse they sang the earth into existence.

They sang the rivers and the trees into vibrant, flowing splendor. They sang the oceans full of fish and the heavens full of birds. They sang every living, breathing, moving, towering, tiny, spacious, magnificent, microscopic thing on the earth into vibrant reality. And when they had circled and sung every corner of the globe, they began the trek back to their sleeping places. As they did, their singing echoed back to them, and it was clear that every melody of the song that was the earth had a place to call home . . . except for one.

One lone melody was unembodied. It had no home like all the others. And it felt lost and confused. "Where do I belong?" it cried to the ancient Ancestors as they entered back into the earth. "Why am I not a river or an ocean or a mountain or a dove? Where do I belong? Tell me what I am."

The Ancestors were too tired from their journey to answer the cries of this lone melody, but the Sky Dwellers were still circling the newest song in the universe, and so the melody sought direction from them.

> *Tell me where I belong. Surely you understand.*
> *I cannot be myself until I find out who I am.*
> *Is there a place for me? Is there a master plan?*
> *I need to know where I belong.*

The melody waited patiently for an answer. The Sky Dwellers gave the melody this simple counsel:

Harmony, harmony, it's harmony, my friend!
Harmonize with earth and sky and everything therein.
If you want to find yourself,
You've got to harmonize with something else.
The only way to reach your goal
Of finding your own soul
Is to harmonize with earth,
Sun and moon and stars.
And when you find sweet harmony,
You're going to find out who you are!

Once the counsel was given and repeated so it couldn't be misunderstood, the Sky Dwellers vanished into the heavens. The melody was left alone to unlock the mystery of what the Sky Dwellers had said.

Descending back to the earth, the melody searched its own essence to understand what it was to do—how it was going to find its place in the orchestration of all things. To harmonize, the melody reasoned, I must first *listen.*

And so it did. It listened long and deep to the songs that lived across the land and sea. It listened to the faintest humming of delicate wild flowers and to the droning constancy of the rushing rivers. It heard everything from the bugling antlered ones to the bellowing furry ones, and the journey continued to the tops of the mountains and the depths of the seas. As it was ascending from the ocean floor, the unembodied melody heard something it hadn't heard before—a song of danger and fear.

It was sung by a barramundi fish, hiding beneath a seaweed that wasn't quite big enough to disguise its quivering fins. The barramundi was starving itself to death, frightened at the prospect of searching for food in the open waters because it had recently watched a brother fish disappear into the massive jaws of a saltwater crocodile.

It's a dangerous and frightening world out there.
I have seen what it can do to one who enters unprepared.
It can take your hopes and dreams,
Blow them all to smithereens!
It's a dangerous and frightening world out there!

There are monsters that are hungry for the kill.
And the innocent are reticent
To think the monsters will.
But they're everywhere you turn,
And they're scary, and I've learned
It's a dangerous and frightening world out there!

And so I'll be remaining safely confined to this space.
My friends say that I'll starve to death in a while
If I don't venture out of this place.

But it's a dangerous and frightening world out there.
And to live a life therein is such a perilous affair.
I'll be safe and I'll be sound
Buried underneath the ground,
'Cause it's a dangerous and frightening world out there!
It's a dangerous and frightening world out there!

The melody felt uncontrollably drawn to the frightened fish and listened to the anguish of its song. And then, without even thinking about it, the melody wrapped itself around the strains of fear and created . . . *harmony!* The barramundi song began to transform, as if being led from the prison of its own fear by the presence of the new melody. Stanzas of courage began to silence the whimpering of despair, and a new song, a new creature, was born.

Because it's clear,
Because you're here,
Because your love is drowning the fear—
Because I thirst
To quench the hurt,
Because not trying is always worse,

I will not be afraid.
I will not run away.
I'll face the music gladly that I have made.
I will not be afraid.
I will not be afraid.

For so long I chose to be
A prisoner of fear.
I prolonged the slavery
For too many years, for too many years.

I will not be afraid.
I will not run away.
I'll grow a little stronger every day.
I'll let the memories of failure fade.
And the things I've learned, I will not trade.
I will not be afraid.
I will not run away.

I'm going to try a little harder, come what may.
I'll face the music proudly that I have made.
If you knew me then, you'll know I've changed today.
I will not be afraid. I will not run away.
I will not be afraid. I will not run away.
I will not be afraid. I will not be afraid.

The melody felt life rush through it. Anticipation filled its being. It felt certain it was going to be darting through the sea as a companion and fellow barramundi.

The melody waited for its birth as a fish, but it never came. *How could this be?* the melody pondered. *I found such harmony. I felt my destiny come rushing over me. Yet all I seem to be is a distant serenade.*

If it wasn't going to be a barramundi, the melody saw no reason to remain in the sea, so it bolted for the sky and soared the heavens, where only the clouds could sing their song. On its journey from cloud to passing cloud, the melody was drawn to an ever so faint tune coming from a nest in a lonely tree. The melody approached and heard the saddest refrain. It came from a white-breasted sea eagle calling for its mother.

> *Perhaps today she's coming home.*
> *Why won't she return?*
> *I search the place I last saw her face,*
> *And the ache within me burns.*
> *I've told myself a thousand times*
> *She's in heaven's hand.*
> *But where could she be needed more than here by me?*
> *Though I try I can't understand*
> *Why she's not coming home*
> *And I'm left all alone.*

The melancholy tune of the sea eagle was literally smothering the poor baby bird. The melody felt compelled to descend as if it were a mother eagle returning to the nest to protect its young.

The melody did more than protect, however. It healed the broken song and gave it hope and renewal. It was this harmonizing melody that enabled the sea eagle to sing a new song, to raise itself from the depths of its own despair and soar!

I feel something strangely familiar,
Gentle as the morning dew,
Reaching out to ease my sadness
Like someone who's known lonely too.

Maybe they have been forsaken,
And they're wandering aimlessly,
Searching for a lost companion,
Needing someone just like me.

Who'd have thought that I could be needed?
Who'd have dreamed someday I'd fly
With these wings I thought were broken
Higher than I ever dared to try?

The sea eagle was magically lifted out of its nest and onto the currents of wind. As the bird found fulfillment in flight, the melody that had made it possible felt completely connected and whole.

I'll be joining the young eagle any moment, the melody thought, *with wings of my own. Together we'll soar, high and strong and swift and free.*

The incarnation of the melody as a sea eagle never came, though the melody waited a long time. It started analyzing and philosophizing and questioning the fairness of the universe. The melody felt cheated, not simply because it hadn't been born with an identity or a specific place to dwell, a mortal home of its own, but also because the Sky Dwellers had deceived it. The melody *had* been harmonizing with the earth, yet it was no closer to finding out who or what it was than before the journey had begun.

In protest and rebellion, the melody began to chant, "It isn't fair. Life really isn't fair. There is no justice anywhere. Nothing in life is fair!" The melody became dark and

despairing—not unlike the barramundi and the sea eagle before their songs were changed. The anger of the melody fed on itself, growing louder and louder and louder, until—it heard an echo. But there were no canyon walls nearby to make one. Where was the echo coming from? The melody stopped completely for a moment and just listened. It was not an echo it was hearing. Something or someone was singing the same angry song. *This was all part of the plan,* the melody reasoned. *Had it not been for the experience with the barramundi and the sea eagle, I would never have sung the song of anger and despair that led me to this kindred spirit. Whoever it is that sings with* me *will be the one who can tell me what I am.*

The melody drew closer to the angry chanting and saw a young man sitting on a log, tearing up a memento of his lost love. He ripped each piece of the parchment in rhythm with his song, throwing the pieces into the air. When his song could find no more anger, it collapsed into a song of love lost. It was a song without words.

As the melody listened, it sensed that the strains of love lost were more haunting than anything else it had ever heard or could imagine hearing. Hearing another's sorrow melted away the melody's own anger and disappointment, which seemed insignificant in comparison.

From the depths of the young man's soul came the song of someone who was lost . . . lost without love. It was as if he was only half a being without his love. *Oh,* the melody thought, *if only I could be his love. If only I could be his other half!*

The sheer longing of the melody caused it to embrace the young man's melancholy melody. And as it did, there was fire and passion and tenderness all at the same time. The melody's only thought was to fill the song's aching empty spaces, to lift and heal and bless and feel. To love.

As the melody gave its all to comfort and love the grieving man, it forgot about itself completely. The melody never imagined what it was starting to learn: that finding one's true self must require losing one's self first. And this it did. It became lost in a song that began in discord but triumphed through the sweetest harmony of all—that of true love.

The melody felt totally at peace for the first time in its existence, and it felt certain that it would awake, as if from a dream, to find itself as the true love of the young man. But that was not to be. The melody lingered in his presence for some time—long enough,

in fact, to see that the new song he was singing brought such new light into his soul that he drew a beautiful true companion to him, and in time they were married and brought many new songs to the earth.

The melody was confused. How could it have learned so much and yet discovered so little about itself? It sought a final audience with the Oldest and Wisest of Sky Dwellers. It sent its melodic request into space with all the energy it could muster, then waited for a reply. The reply came only when the melody was finally ready to hear it: "You have harmonized with the earth and everything that's in it, and yet you still don't know who you are?" The Sky Dweller asked with a hint of bewilderment in its heavenly voice.

"I have tried. With everything I am, I have tried, and yet I've failed. It's strange, because at the time I thought I had harmonized with the frightened barramundi, yet I did not join the fish and roam the seas. For a few moments I could have sworn I found harmony with the orphaned sea eagle, yet I did not grow wings and join it in flight. And I felt the nearest thing I've known to love with the young man, but my melody must not have been good enough or I would have found myself at his side forever."

The Sky Dweller listened patiently but still shook his head in disbelief. "Can't you see? Isn't it clear what you are? After all you have done, must I tell you?"

"Oh, please," the melody begged, "please, and I will be the very best of whatever it is you tell me I am."

"Of that I have no doubt," the Sky Dweller said, and then paused. He motioned for the melody to come as close as it could. Then he whispered slowly and lovingly, *"You are a melody! Not a fish or a bird or a mountain or a stream. A melody! What a rare and precious thing you are! Just think of where you've been, what you've learned, how you've felt. These things are treasures, you know. Of course there have been moments of sadness and*
sorrow, but you felt *them, deeply, because you had an extraordinary capacity to feel. Be grateful that there are things you care so deeply about. And be grateful that you have been willing to use your gift to help those around you. It has been that caring that has brought courage to the fearful, hope to the disheartened, and love to the lonely."*

"Not me," the melody protested. "I didn't do anything special. I was just being . . . myself."

"*Listen to yourself*," the Sky Dweller said with emphasis. "Listen to yourself! You were just being what *only* you can be—a melody! And you worked miracles simply by being yourself. Unfortunately, most of us can't believe that by being who we are we make any difference at all. But oh, we do!

"Remember how you felt when you'd given the best you had to another? Remember that feeling, always. It will serve you well when you yourself become discouraged. And always remember that you are loved, loved for what you alone have the unique power to be and do. So why would you ever want to be anything else but what you are?

There is a place here that only you can fill.
And this empty space awaits the magic you instill.
For your warm embrace does what nothing else can do.
You're second to none because you're the one and only you.

Something was missing until you came along.
And someone's been wishing you would fill their heart with song.
For no other melody can touch them like you do.
Their song goes unsung if not for the one and only you.

So don't waste your energy
Chasing a destiny
You were not sent here to claim.
That isn't the reason you came,
And you know that it's true.
You cannot truly be anything else,
So reach for the best in yourself.
You're more than a miracle;
You're the original you!

And if you should wonder if this could be the truth,
The hearts you have lifted up are more than living proof.
And if you are listening, a message is coming through
With thanks from above and love for the one and only you.

As the Sky Dweller drifted away, he called out to the melody, "I want you to sing proudly and humbly at the same moment: 'I am a melody! I have always been and will always be wondrous and wonderful!' "

For no other melody can touch me like you do.
And this song is sung with love for the one and only you.

As Aunt Louise finished the story, they were almost home. The stars filled the sky so densely that Ellie thought she saw the shapes of the Sky Dwellers smiling down on them.

"Thank you, Aunt Louise, for the story."

Louise looked off into the distance and said, "And I thank you, my Aboriginal friend, for a gift to pass on to my . . . daughter."

"By any chance did she sing you the melody when she told you the story, Aunt Louise?"

Louise became very still and looked as if she was fighting to keep her composure. "She did . . ."

Louise began to hum something. A moment later, Ellie began humming along. It was the tune she had hummed earlier that day, the melody that Louise recognized as the signal that Ellie was ready.

"I know this song!" Ellie interrupted. "But how do I know it?"

Louise just kept humming. She wanted to give the melody a chance to work its magic before she spoke. Then, with a single tear in her eye, Louise explained: "All the women in our family know this tune. You heard it from your mother when she was singing you to sleep as a child, just as she and I heard it from our mother who was in the kitchen scrubbing the floor. And you know, Ellie, she probably heard that same simple melody hummed by her mother as she did the ironing late at night. And that woman received the melody from a wonderful woman as she rocked the cradle, singing her to sleep, or as she milked the goats or shucked the corn or did any of the ordinary things women do for those they love. And just like the melody in the story, these remarkable women have blessed and touched lives, perhaps without ever knowing what an incredible gift they were giving just by being themselves."

Louise's voice became softer and softer as if she were drifting back through the generations and thanking every woman who had hummed that distant serenade. She looked deep into her niece's eyes, tenderly took her face in her hands, and said, "I've spent my whole life searching for something I already had—a legacy passed from generation to generation by strong, loving women. I've had something as precious as any story told around tribal fires. I was sung to, and in the singing came a simple emotional imprint of all the truly important things anyone could ever hope to carry through life—compassion, understanding, forgiveness, inspiration, example, service, strength, and love . . ."

Louise could speak no more. Her heart was too full, and the words failed to communicate all she was feeling, so she simply held her niece tightly and enjoyed a special harmony under the starry Australian sky.

The tenderness of that evening lasted Ellie for a long time. She would cling to its memory when the waves of melancholy washed over her like an uncontrollable tide. At those moments when she felt herself slipping on the edge of despair, she heard a melody, as if coming from the next room, hummed softly and reassuringly first by one woman, then joined by another and

another until it was a chorus sung by all the women who had passed the melody of their lives from generation to generation to generation.

When there is no one near,
When you feel lost and afraid,
Listen and you will hear
A distant serenade.

Voices from long ago
Aren't really so far away.
They'll heal an aching soul
With their distant serenade.

It's a melody that keeps on beckoning:
"Comfort one another.
Be what only you can be.
Strengthen each other."

Maybe the time will come
When you'll join an eternal parade
Of all the lives who've loved and sung
A distant serenade.

TELL ME WHERE I BELONG

Words and Music by
MICHAEL McLEAN

HARMONY

Words and Music by
MICHAEL McLEAN

Har - mo - ny, har - mo - ny,___ it's har - mo - ny, my friend!___

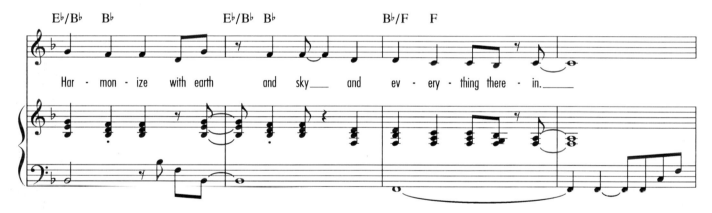

Har - mon - ize with earth and sky___ and ev - ery - thing there - in.___

If you want to find your - self,___ You've got to har - mon - ize with some - thing else.___ The on - ly way to reach

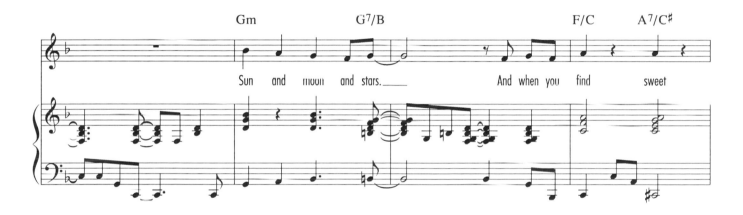

IT'S A DANGEROUS AND FRIGHTENING WORLD

Words and Music by
MICHAEL McLEAN

It's a

dan - ger - ous___ and fright - en - ing___ world out there.___
mon - sters that are hun - gry for the kill.___
dan - ger - ous___ and fright - en - ing___ world out there.___

I have seen what___ it can do to one who
And the in - no - cent___ are re - ti - cent To
And to live a life___ there - in is

32

safe - ly__ con - fined to this space. My friends say that I'll__ starve to death

D.S. 𝄋 al Coda ⊕

in a while__ If I don't ven - ture out of this place. But it's a

⊕ *Coda*

there. It's a dan - ger - ous__ and fright - 'ning world_____ out there!

I WILL NOT BE AFRAID

Words and Music by
MICHAEL McLEAN and JOHN BATDORF

ALL ALONE

Words and Music by
MICHAEL McLEAN

Per - haps to - day she's com - ing home. Why won't she re - turn?____ I
I've told my - self a thou - sand times She's in heav - en's hand.____ But

search the place I last saw her face, And the ache with - in me burns.
where could she be need - ed more than here by me? Tho' I try I can't un - der -

stand Why she's not com - ing home and I'm left all a - lone.

Something Strangely Familiar

Words and Music by
MICHAEL McLEAN

Ballad ♩ = 60-70

I feel some-thing___ strange-ly fa-mil-iar,___ Gen-tle as the morn-ing dew,
May-be they have___ been for-sak-en, And they're wan-dering aim-less-ly,

Reach-ing out to___ ease my sad-ness___ Like some-one___ who's known lone-ly too.
Search-ing for a___ lost com-pan-ion,___ Need-ing___ some-one___

just like me. Who'd have thought that I could be need-ed?___ Who'd have dreamed some-day I'd fly___

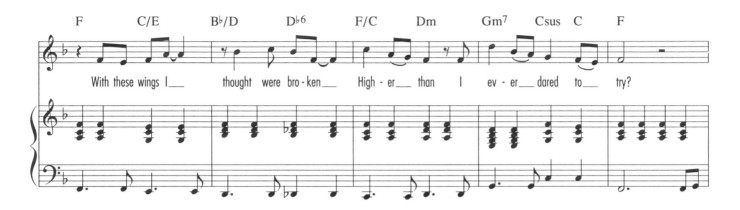

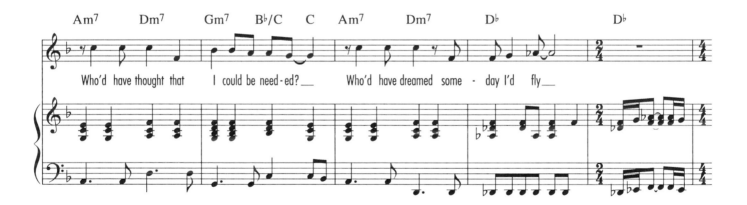

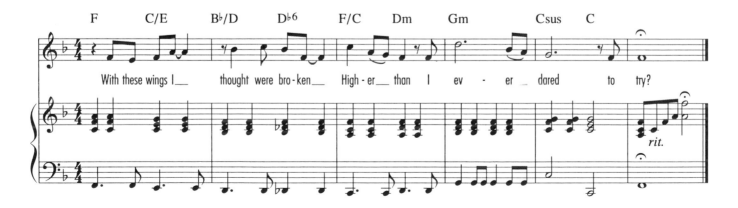

SONG WITHOUT WORDS

Music by
MICHAEL McLEAN

THE ONE AND ONLY YOU

Words and Music by
MICHAEL McLEAN

There is a place here that on-ly you can fill. And this em-pty space a-waits the
miss-ing un-til you came a-long. And some-one's been wish-ing you would

ma-gic you in-still. For your warm em-brace does what noth-ing else___can do. You're se-cond to none be-cause you're the one and on-ly
fill their heart with song. For no oth-er mel-o-dy can touch them like___you do. Their song goes un-sung if not for the one and on-ly

you.
you.

Some-thing was

So don't waste your e-ner-gy Chas-ing a des-ti-ny

Words and Music by
MICHAEL McLEAN

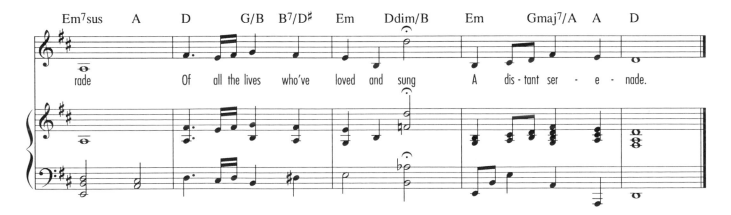